The Finger-Eater

Books by the same author

Aristotle
Clever Lollipop
Lady Lollipop
My Animal Friends
Sophie Hits Six
Sophie in the Saddle
Sophie Is Seven
Sophie's Lucky
Sophie's Snail
Sophie's Tom

The Finger-Eater

Dick King-Smith
Illustrated by Arthur Robins

WALKER
BOOKS

For Gareth

A. R.

First published 1992 by Walker Books Ltd
87 Vauxhall Walk, London SE11 5HJ

This edition published 2017

2 4 6 8 10 9 7 5 3 1

Text © 1992 Fox Busters Ltd
Illustrations © 1992, 2001 Arthur Robins

The right of Dick King-Smith and Arthur Robins to be identified as author
and illustrator respectively of this work has been asserted by them
in accordance with the Copyright, Designs and Patents Act 1988

This book has been typeset in Garamond

Printed in Great Britain by Clays Ltd, St Ives plc

British Library Cataloguing in Publication Data:
a catalogue record for this book is available from the British Library

ISBN 978-0-7445-5994-1

www.walker.co.uk

Contents

Chapter One

Long long ago, in the cold lands
of the North, there lived a most
unusual troll.

Like all the hill-folk (so called
because they usually made their
homes in holes in the hills) he was
hump-backed and bow-legged,
with a frog-face and bat-ears and
razor-sharp teeth.

But he grew up (though, like all
other trolls, not very tall) with an
extremely bad habit –

he liked to eat fingers!

Ulf (for that was his name) always
went about this in the same way.

Whenever he spied someone walking
alone on the hills, he would come up,
smiling broadly, and hold out a hand,
and say politely:

"How do you do?"

Now trolls are usually rude and
extremely grumpy and don't care
how anyone does, so the person
would be pleasantly surprised at
meeting such a jolly one, and
would hold out his or her
hand to shake Ulf's.

Then Ulf would take it and, quick
as a flash, bite off a finger with his
razor-sharp teeth and run away as
fast as his bow-legs would carry him,
chewing like mad and grinning all
over his frog-face.

Strangers visiting those parts were amazed to see how many men, women and children were lacking a finger on their right hands, especially children, because their fingers were more tender and much sought after by Ulf.

Nobody lacked more than one finger, because even small children weren't foolish enough to shake hands if they met Ulf a second time, but ran away with them deep in their pockets.

It was usually the index finger
that Ulf nipped off because it was
the easiest to get at, so that many
children grew up pointing with a
middle finger...

and holding a pencil between middle
and third...

but sometimes Ulf went for the little
one: thumbs, for some reason, he
did not seem to fancy.

Strangely, the people of those lands
were tolerant and long-suffering and
seemed to put up with Ulf's bad habit.

"What can't be cured must be
endured," they would say, and since
they considered it was no use crying
over spilt milk, they wasted no tears
over lost fingers but got on with their
lives with only seven.

Chapter Two

Who knows how long Ulf the troll
might have continued in his wicked
ways if it had not been for a little girl
named Gudrun.

Gudrun was the only child of a reindeer farmer. She had golden hair which she wore in a long plait, and eyes the colour of cornflowers.

Indeed she was as pretty as a picture, looking as though reindeer butter wouldn't melt in her mouth.

She was also a sensible child, who
paid attention to what her parents
told her.

One evening, as they all sat round
the fire outside their tent, Gudrun's
mother said to her:

Remember, you
must never shake
hands with a troll.

She stirred the cooking-pot that was suspended above the flames. The hand that held the ladle had no little finger.

With his right hand, on which the index finger was missing, Gudrun's father picked up a stick to put on the fire.

25

"But why," said Gudrun, "didn't either of you do that?"

"When we were both children," said her mother, "we didn't know about the Finger-eater."

"We were among the first in this district," said her father, "to lose a finger. But now everybody knows."

"Why don't all the mothers and fathers warn their children then?" said Gudrun.

"They do," said her mother, "but sometimes the children don't listen, or they just forget. Mind you remember."

Gudrun thought deeply about this while she was out on the hills, helping her father herd his reindeer as they grazed their way across the slopes.

It's all very well, she thought, to tell children not to get their fingers eaten, but someone ought to tell that troll not to eat them. Eating people's fingers is wrong.

And being not only a very pretty but also a very resolute child, she resolved that she would stop the Finger-eater. But how?

"Father," she said as she sat milking one of the reindeer, "how big is a troll?"

"No taller than you, Gudrun," her father said, "but much much stronger."

"Have you ever met one?"

For answer her father held up his
right hand.

"Oh yes," said Gudrun. "But since then, I mean?"

"No," said her father, "but I have quite often seen the hill-folk, just for

a moment. Then they scuttle down
their holes, for they are all shy of
people. Except Ulf the Finger-eater."

"You have never seen him again?"
"No, and nor will you, I hope."
But not long after, Gudrun did.

Chapter Three

Even in those bleak Northern lands
there are days in the short summer
which are bright and warm and
flower-filled, and on such a morning

Gudrun's father handed her a flask.
It was made of reindeer skin, was this
flask, and it was stopped with a cork
made out of reindeer horn, and
it was filled with fresh, rich
reindeer milk.

"Be a good girl and take this to your mother," her father said, for the herd's grazing grounds were not far from the family tent, and it did not occur to him that she might come to any harm.

Gudrun set off across the hill,
carrying the flask in her right hand.
Before she had gone far she saw,
in a steep bank, a large hole.

Could that be the home of one of
the hill-folk? she thought, and no
sooner had she thought it than out
of the hole came a hump-backed,
bow-legged figure with a frog-face
and bat-ears.

Straight towards her he came, his mouth agape in a friendly smile, his hand outstretched. "How do you do?" he said politely.

The Finger-eater! thought Gudrun and she remembered her parents' advice to put her hands in her pockets and run. But I won't, she said to herself bravely, for now may be my only chance to make the Finger-eater see how wrong it is to eat fingers. So she stood her ground.

"I'm sorry," she said, "but I cannot shake your hand because I'm holding this flask of milk."

"You could always hold it with your other hand," said Ulf, for it was he.

"I could," said Gudrun, "but I
won't. I've heard of you, you see.
You are Ulf the Finger-eater."

"Well, well," said Ulf, passing his
tongue across his razor-sharp teeth,
"and what is your name, little girl?"

"It's Gudrun. Now let me tell you something, Ulf," she said. "Eating fingers is wrong."

A clever little miss, thought Ulf. How can I trick her? He sat down on a nearby tree-stump, and crossed one bow-leg over the other, looking serious and thoughtful.

"You're right, Gudrun," he said.
"I'm wrong to eat people's fingers,
I see that now. But at least give me
a drink of milk."

And when she holds out the flask,
he thought, I'll soon have one of
those lovely little pink sausages!

"Not on your life," said Gudrun.
"Thanks to you, both my mother
and my father are short of a finger."

"How time flies!" said Ulf. "That
must have been when I was a very
young troll. I've probably had a
hundred fingers since then."

"Well, you're not having a hundred and one," said Gudrun, "but on second thoughts I'll give you that drink," and pulling out the cork, she jerked the flask so that the milk shot out straight into Ulf's frog-face, and as he stood gasping, she dashed away.

Chapter Four

Gudrun did not tell her parents of her meeting with Ulf. She simply said she had tripped, the cork had come out of the flask, and the milk had all spilled (a white lie, she told herself).

But she continued to think long
and hard about the Finger-eater.
Somehow or other he must be made
to give up his horrid habit.

Then one day Gudrun had a
sudden, brilliant idea.

She was sitting outside the family
tent, playing with a reindeer antler.
This was the time of year when all the
reindeer (for the cows are horned as
well as the bulls) shed their antlers

before growing fresh ones, and they
were lying about everywhere. Hard
as iron they were, and many of
them were of the strangest shapes,
for reindeer antlers are very large
and many-pointed, those of some
of the bulls curving right
round and down until
they almost meet the
animals' faces.

The single antler that Gudrun held was quite a small one, probably from a young beast, but at its tip it had an odd shape, something like a human hand. It had at its end a flat surface resembling the palm of a hand and from this surface five points protruded. Just like four fingers and a thumb, thought Gudrun, and that was when the idea hit her.

That afternoon Ulf emerged from his hole to see Gudrun approaching, her long blonde plait swinging as she walked, her cornflower-blue eyes sparkling, her right hand, much to the troll's surprise, already outstretched in greeting. Admittedly she was wearing a large pair of reindeer hide gloves, but those won't save her, thought Ulf.

He advanced to meet her.

"Hello, Ulf," said Gudrun brightly.
"I've come to say I'm sorry for
throwing the milk at you. Will you
shake hands and then we can be
friends?"

Stupid child, thought Ulf. She's asking for it. This time I won't just have one finger, I'll have all four, and he grabbed Gudrun's right hand and shoved it into his frog-mouth and bit it as hard as he could.

Then Ulf's great cry of agony
echoed and rang from the
circling hills, as
his razor-
sharp teeth
broke
and
smashed
and
shattered,
every one.
And Gudrun
drew off the mangled glove
that had concealed the antler,
its stem thrust up the sleeve of
her blouse, and revealed that bony
five-pointed end that had looked so
like a hand.

"Hard luck, Ulf," she said. "You bit off more than you could chew."

"Oh! Oh!" moaned the Finger-eater. "My teeth! My teeth! Every single one is loose in my head! Oh, it is agony! Help me! Help me!"

"I will," said Gudrun, and she took
from the pocket of her skirt a pair of
stout pliers, a useful tool with which
her father was wont to draw stones
that had lodged deep between the
great splay hooves of his reindeer.

"Open wide, Ulf," she said, "and I'll
make you a much better troll."

Then with the pliers she pulled
out the teeth of the Finger-eater,
one by one, till none were left.

Chapter Five

Even after that, Ulf could not easily
rid himself of his bad habit.

Once his mouth was no longer sore, he still tried several times to live up to his name, but thanks to Gudrun, he could not. For though the reindeer can grow new antlers, hill-folk cannot grow new teeth, and those few people whose hands he caught only giggled at the harmless pressure of his toothless gums upon their fingers and told him not to be such a silly old troll.

So that before long Ulf fell into a terrible sulk, and disappeared down his hole in the hill, and was never seen again.

And even today, if you travel in the cold old North and stay amongst the reindeer people, you may hear the tale of the troll named Ulf and the girl called Gudrun, and how she and she alone put paid to the wicked ways of the Finger-eater.

Dick King-Smith (1922–2011), a former dairy farmer, is one of the world's favourite children's book authors. Winner of the Guardian Children's Fiction Prize for *The Sheep-pig* (filmed as *Babe*), he was named Children's Book Author of the Year in 1991 and won the 1995 Children's Book Award for *Harriet's Hare*. His titles for Walker include *Aristotle*, *Lady Lollipop* and its sequel, *Clever Lollipop*, *My Animal Friends*, and the much-loved Sophie series.